D0501603

CALGARY PUBLIC LIBRARY

JAN - - 2013

VAMPIRE SCHOOL

Teacher Screecher

For Theo and Tara
P.B.
For my Mum
C.H.

Library of Congress Cataloging-in-Publication Data

Bently, Peter, 1960-
Teacher screecher / by Peter Bently ; illustrated by Chris Harrison.
p. cm.—(Vampire school)
Summary: When Lee and his vampire friends get
a monster for a substitute teacher, they investigate
why she is not as nice as she was when she taught at
the werewolf primary school their friend Ollie attends.
ISBN 978-0-8075-8466-8 (hardcover)
ISBN 978-0-8075-8467-5 (pbk.)
[1. Substitute teachers—Fiction. 2. Monsters—Fiction.
3. School—Fiction. 4. Vampires—Fiction. 5. Werewolves—Fiction.]
I. Harrison, Chris, ill. II. Title.
PZ7.B4475424Te 2012
[Fic]—dc23
2011045128

Based on an original idea by Chris Harrison.
Text copyright © 2010 Peter Bently.
Illustrations copyright © 2010 Chris Harrison.
Published in 2012 by Albert Whitman & Company.
All rights reserved. No part of this book may be reproduced or
transmitted in any form or by any means, electronic or mechanical,
including photocopying, recording, or by any information storage
and retrieval system, without permission in writing from the
publisher. Printed in the United States of America.

10 9 8 7 6 5 4 3 2 1 ML 16 15 14 13 12

For more information about Albert Whitman & Company,
visit our web site at www.albertwhitman.com.

VAMPIRE SCHOOL

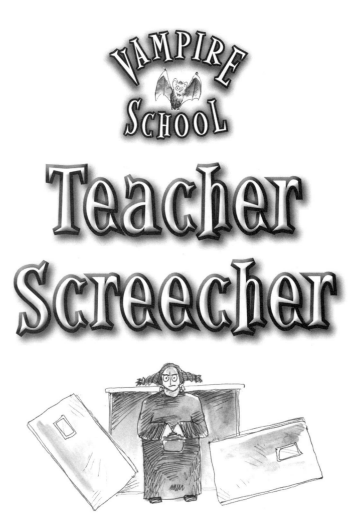

Teacher Screecher

Written by **Peter Bently**

Illustrated by **Chris Harrison**

Albert Whitman & Company
Chicago, Illinois

Contents

Chapter 1
Bat Flu

One evening, Lee Price's mom walked into his bedroom and stopped. The bedroom looked empty.

"Hurry up, you three—wherever you are," said Mrs. Price. "It's twenty to nine.

You'll be late for school!"

"We're in here," said Lee's voice from the wardrobe. "We've all turned into bats. Hang on."

Lee fluttered out of the wardrobe followed by his best

friends, Bella Williams and Billy Pratt.

"We were doing some skulking practice," said Lee.

Lee, Bella, and Billy went to St. Orlok's Primary School for young vampires. Their teacher, Miss Gargoyle, taught them important vampire skills, like cloak swishing and scary staring and how to change into bats.

"Right," said Mrs. Price. "Now off to school. Dad's asleep in bed with bat flu so

it'll be quieter if you leave
through the window."

Mrs. Price opened the
bedroom window and Lee,
Billy, and Bella flew out into
the night. Ten minutes later,
they flapped through the
school gates and changed back
into vampire form.

A strange black van was parked nearby. On the side of the van it said:

Frances and Kenneth Styne & Company

The driver was helping Mr. Eric Gore, the school's zombie caretaker, lug an enormous crate out of the van. The crate

was nearly ten feet long.

"Frances and Kenneth Styne," said Lee. "I think that's a shop in town. I wonder what's in the crate?"

Mr. Gore looked at them gloomily.

"Vouldn't you like to know, eh?" he droned. "Nosy little vampire brats!"

"Er—good morning, Mr. Gore," said Lee as politely as

he could.

"Ye-e-e-s!" groaned Mr. Gore, patting the crate. "Oh yes. A very good mornink indeed!"

He opened his mouth and made a weird noise like someone coughing, gargling, and throwing up all at the same time.

"Hrurgh! Hrurgh! Hrurgh!"

"Good grief," whispered Lee. "Old Gore's actually laughing!"

"Wow!" said Billy. "Do you think he's sick? There's a lot of bat flu about."

"Don't be silly," said Bella. "Only

vampires get bat flu. And bats, of course."

"So why is he so cheerful?" said Billy. "Old Gore doesn't do cheerful."

"I bet it's something to do with that crate," said Lee. "Maybe it's a new floor polisher. He's always moaning about the old one."

Lee was right. It was something to do with the crate. But it wasn't a new floor polisher. Inside the crate was something much, much worse.

Chapter 2
Miss Fitt

Lee, Bella, and Billy entered their classroom to see Mrs. Garlick, the school principal.

"Settle down, please, Miss Gargoyle's class!" said Mrs. Garlick. "I am afraid Miss Gargoyle has a nasty case of bat flu. She will be off school for at least two weeks."

"Oh, poor Miss Gargoyle!" said Bella.

"While Miss Gargoyle is away, you will have a substitute teacher," said Mrs Batty. "She has also worked at Chaney Street Elementary School and Mr. Savage, the principal, tells me that she is very nice." Chaney Street was the werewolf elementary school down the road. "In fact, she should be here any min—"

She was interrupted by a noise in the corridor.

STOMP!

STOMP!
STOMP!
STOMP!

"Yikes!" said Lee, as the whole classroom shook. "What on earth is that?"

STOMP!
STOMP!
STOMP!

The heavy stomping sound
was getting louder and louder.
And closer and closer.

STOMP!
STOMP!
STOMP!

Tables wobbled and windows
rattled. Pencils and crayons
jumped out of pots.

Mrs. Garlick's glasses fell off her nose. The Monster Munches that Big Herb was secretly eating bounced out of the packet and onto the floor.

STOMP!

STOMP!

STOMP!

The noise stopped. Everyone held their breath. Then—

CRUNCH!
SPLINTER!
CRACK!

The classroom door was torn off its hinges. It toppled to the ground with a

KER-RASH!

But the young vampires weren't looking at the door.

They were looking at what was standing in the doorway.

It was ten feet tall and five feet wide. It was dressed completely in black and clutched a little pink handbag. Two stiff braids stuck out horizontally from its head. And two steel bolts stuck out horizontally from its neck.

Attached to one of the bolts was a label that said:

PROPERTY OF
F. AND K. STYNE & CO.

It was a monster. The children gasped.

"Now we know what was in that crate!" whispered Lee.

"SILENCE!"

roared the monster.

Mrs. Garlick smiled nervously.

"Ah, children," she said. "Erm—allow me to introduce Miss Fitt. Your new teacher."

Chapter 3

Number Nightmare

As Mrs. Garlick slipped hastily out of the room, Miss Fitt lurched to the front of the classroom like a walking earthquake. She turned and slowly stared around the class.

"SILENCE!"

she bellowed, even though it was so quiet, you could hear

a pin drop. "There will be no noise in my class! Now get out your math books!"

A flutter of grumbles went around the room.

"SILENCE!"

hollered Miss Fitt.

Bella put her hand up.

"Please, miss," she said. "We have vampire history now, not math. We don't have math till after break."

"SILENCE!"

screeched Miss Fitt. "If I say
we have math, we have math!
What is your name, girl?"

"B-Bella Williams, miss."

"What is thirty-seven times
thirty-seven? You have five
seconds!" demanded Miss Fitt.

Bella was really good at
math and was about to give
the answer when Miss Fitt
snapped, "Time's up! Hah!
As I thought! Vampires know
nothing! You will all stay in
during break and write out

your thirty-seven times table
thirty-seven times!"

"Aw, miss!" groaned the

class.

"SILENCE!"

roared Miss Fitt. "Never
speak with your mouth open!
Vampires should be seen and
not heard! And preferably not
seen either!"

Lee, Bella, and Billy swapped glances.

"No wonder old Gore was so happy!" whispered Lee.

"SILENCE!

Vampires are a lazy bunch of ghoul-for-nothings! Lying around in coffins all day when they could be doing MATH!"

Grabbing a red marker pen, Miss Fitt stomped up to the big timetable on the classroom wall.

"I'm not teaching any of this useless vampire nonsense.

Vampire history indeed!"

She drew a thick line through vampire history and wrote MATH instead.

"And what's this? Bat lessons?" spat Miss Fitt. "Ridiculous! If

vampires were meant to fly they would have wings already, without any of this changing into bats rubbish!"

So out went bat lessons and in went—more MATH.

By the time Miss Fitt had finished, the timetable looked like this:

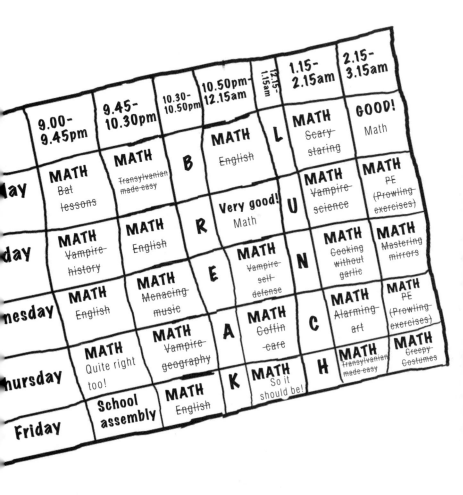

Chapter 4
Monster Mystery

"I don't understand," said Billy. "Mrs. Garlick said Miss Fitt would be nice."

"That's only what the principal at Chaney Street told her," said Lee.

"But why would he say it if it wasn't true?" said Bella. "Mrs. Garlick could have easily found someone else."

"I know," said Lee. "Let's ask Ollie after school." Ollie Talbot was Lee's werewolf friend at Chaney Street.

"Good idea," agreed Bella.

"He always walks home past the school gate. If we leave on time, we can catch him."

Unfortunately Bella spoke too soon. During the very last lesson of the night—

math instead of PE (prowling exercises)—Billy accidentally squashed Bella's toe with his chair leg.

"Ouch!" cried Bella. "Careful, Billy!"

"SILENCE!"

screeched Miss Fitt. "So. Bella Williams. You again, eh? I might have known!"

"But miss—" Bella tried to explain.

"SILENCE!"

"It wasn't her fault, miss," said Billy.

"SILENCE!"

cried Miss Fitt. "I can see you're a pair of regular troublemakers. You will both stay after school and write out 'The square of the hypotenuse is equal to the sum of the squares of the other two sides' two hundred times! Mrs. Garlick will inform your parents of your misbehavior!"

Bella and Billy looked aghast.

"But, miss, it was an
accident!" cried Lee.

"SILENCE!"

shrieked Miss Fitt. "Since
you're so fond of your
delinquent friends, you can join
them in detention!"

Lee, Billy, and Bella came

out of detention an hour after school had ended.

"Oh brother," said Bella. "It's starting to rain."

"And we missed Ollie," grumbled Lee.

"No, we didn't," cried Billy suddenly. "There he is!"

Ollie was just walking past the school. It wasn't a full moon that night, so he looked just like an ordinary boy, apart from his hairy hands.

"Of course," said Lee. "I

forgot he had casketball
practice tonight." Casketball
was a game a bit like
basketball.

"Hey Ollie!" called Lee.

Ollie came over.

"Hi Lee!" he said. "Hi Billy
and Bella! What are you doing
at school so late?"

"Detention," explained

Bella. "Miss Gargoyle's off with bat flu. Until she comes back, we've got a horrible new teacher."

"We were going to ask you about her," said Lee. "Her name's Miss Fitt."

"What?" said Ollie. "Miss Fitt gave you detention? As in Miss Fitt of Styne and Company?"

"That's her," said Lee.

"Wow!" said Ollie, amazed. "We had Miss

Fitt for a month when our teacher broke his hind leg. She was brilliant. She gave us tons of sweets and never got angry!"

This time it was Lee, Bella, and Billy who gasped in amazement.

"But do you know the best thing about her?" Ollie went on. "We did hardly any math. She said it was boring! How cool is that?" He glanced at his watch. "Yikes!

I'll be late for dinner. See you!"

As Ollie hurried off, the three vampires just stood there and gawked. Suddenly, the main school doors opened, and out popped the gloomy, greenish face of Mr. Gore.

He looked at the sky and stuck a grubby hand into the rain, which was falling more heavily now.

"It is startink!" he muttered to himself. "Good! Hrurgh! Hrurgh!" Then he spotted Lee, Bella, and Billy. "Hey! Vot are you doing, you nosy vampire kids? School is closed! Clear off!"

Mr. Gore slammed the door, and the three vampires heard the loud sliding of bolts and the rattling of keys in the lock.

"Come on," said Lee. "I've had enough of school for one night."

"Me too," said Bella. With a *POP! POP! POP!* they all turned into bats.

They were about to head for home when they heard

a horribly familiar noise. It was coming from somewhere behind the school doors:

STOMP! STOMP! STOMP! STOMP!

"Yikes, it's her!" squeaked Billy. "I'm off!"

"Hang on," said Lee. "Didn't old Gore just lock up?"

"Yes," said Billy. "Why?"

"Think about it," said Lee. "If the school is locked for the night, why is Miss Fitt still in the building?"

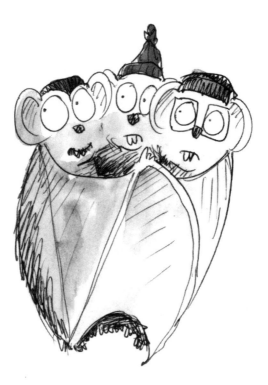

Chapter 5
The Attic

Lee, Billy, and Bella flew up
to the school doors and listened.
"It sounds like she's going
upstairs," said Lee. "Come on!"
They reached the first floor
windows just as Miss Fitt
lumbered onto the landing. But

she didn't stop there. Trailed by the three vampire bats, she climbed the stairs all the way to the top floor. There were no classrooms on this floor, only storerooms. It was a part of St. Orlok's the young vampires had never been to.

"Now what?" said Lee as they skulked under the gutter and out of sight. "There's nowhere else for her to go."

"Not quite," said Billy. "Look!"

Slowly, Miss Fitt crossed the

landing. In one dark and dingy corner was a grimy door. She grabbed the handle and turned it. As the door opened, Lee, Bella, and Billy could clearly read the words on it:

**MR E. GORE
CARETAKER
VAMPIRES KEEP OUT!**

"So that's where old Gore hangs out!" exclaimed Lee. "The attic!"

"But why is she going up there?" cried Bella.

Bella almost had to shout to be heard above the rain. There was a rumble of thunder and a gust of wind, and then a voice behind them suddenly said—

"BOO!"

The vampire bats shrieked and nearly jumped out of their fur. They turned to see Lee's friend Boris, a real bat who lived in the school clock tower.

"Boris!" yelled Lee. "Don't do that!"

"Sorry!" chuckled Boris. "I didn't realize vampires were scared of bats! Tee-hee!"

As he spoke, Miss Fitt lurched through the attic door and slammed it behind her. They heard her stomping up the stairs.

"Hey," said Boris. "Who was that monster?"

"It's Miss Fitt," said Billy. "She's our teacher while Miss Gargoyle is ill."

"Bad luck!" said Boris.
"What's she doing in old
Gore's attic?"

"We'd love to find out," said
Lee.

"No problemo!" said Boris.
"We can use the hole."

"Hole? What hole?" asked Lee.

"I'll show you," said Boris.
"Come on!"

Lee, Bella, and Billy followed
Boris out into the driving
rain and howling wind. They
landed on the roof by a gap
where a tile was missing.

"That's weird," said Lee. "I've
never noticed that hole before."

"It wasn't there until today,"
said Boris. "Old Gore took the
tile out at lunchtime. I saw
him do it."

"Why would
he do that?"
said Lee.

The wind suddenly died down and the four bats heard voices below.

"Ah, Miss Fitt, Miss Fitt! Velcome, velcome!" groaned Gore. "You are looking most elegant zis eefnink!"

"SILENCE, fool!" groaned Miss Fitt. "Hurry! Can't go on . . . much longer . . . Almost . . . run . . . out."

"Do not worry, Miss Fitt, do not worry! Everysink is almost ready! Come over here, and I'll just..."

FLASH!
BOOM!

A great thunderclap made all the bats jump and drowned out the rest of Mr. Gore's words.

"What does he mean?" cried
Lee as the wind picked up
again. "What has Miss Fitt
almost run out of? And what
is almost ready?"

"Why don't we take a look?"
said Boris.

"No way!" said Billy. "Old

Gore's bound
to see us!"
There was
another flash of
lightning, and this
time the thunder was so
loud that the tiles rattled.
"Let's get inside," said Lee.
"It's better than being out in
this storm!"

He peeped over the edge of the hole. "All clear," he said. "Come on!"

One by one they slipped through the hole—and down into old Gore's attic.

Chapter 6

The Monster Megacharger

The four bats dangled in the rafters just under the hole. Gore had his back to them. He appeared to be strapping Miss Fitt to a long black bench surrounded by electrical wires and tubes. These all led to a gigantic machine covered with knobs and switches and dials and lights. A flash of lightning revealed the words on the machine:

MONSTER MEGACHARGER
PROPERTY OF
F. AND K. STYNE & CO.

"Wow," said Boris. "What on earth is that?"

"Well, it isn't a floor polisher, that's for certain," said Lee.

"I don't like the look of it," said Bella.

"I think it's a charging machine," said Billy. "I read about them in *Junior Science Freakly*. They're for recharging

monsters when their power runs out. A bit like a battery charger."

"That's it!" said Bella. "When Miss Fitt said she was 'nearly running out,' she meant she was nearly running out of power. Old Gore's going to recharge her!"

"Come on," said Lee. "Let's go closer while his back is turned."

The bats zipped across the

attic to the cobwebby shadows just above the machine. And not a moment too soon.

FLASh!

flickered the lightning.

BOOM!

crashed the thunder.

Mr. Gore swung around and stared through the hole in the roof.

"Almost time! Almost time!"

he whined. "The weather is perfect!"

"SIIILEEENCE," croaked Miss Fitt, her voice trailing away. "Hurry up, fool!" she rasped.

"Not long now, oh monstrous one!" droned Gore. "When ze lightning is directly overhead, I will give you a super-duper double dose of electricity! After zat it will be no more Miss Nice Monster! Hrurgh! Hrurgh! Hrurgh!"

Mr. Gore clipped a thick

wire to each bolt in Miss Fitt's
neck.

"Yikes," said Lee. "We have
to do something!"

"But what?" said Bella. "I
don't have a clue how that
machine works!"

"Could you work it, Billy?"
asked Boris.

"Er . . . maybe," said Billy.

"If we can get close enough
without old Gore seeing us."

FLASH!
BOOM!

"Almost time! Almost time!"
wailed Mr. Gore, his eyes
wild with joy. "Now for the
lightning conductor!"

Mr. Gore scuttled across the
attic to a shiny metal pole.
There was a brass ball at the
tip and a heavy stand at the
bottom so it wouldn't fall over.
Grunting with effort, Gore
pushed the pole toward the

hole in the roof.

"Quick!" said Lee. "Now's our chance!"

The four bats swooped down to the Monster Megacharger.

"There should be a special knob here somewhere," said Billy, peering at the buzzing, whirring machine with all its flashing dials and buttons and glowing tubes and different colored wires. "Geez! Where is it? It's all very confusing."

FLASH!
BOOM!

"Any second now!"
grunted Mr Gore.
"Hrurgh! Hrurgh!"
The brass tip of the
conductor was now sticking
out of the hole into the storm.
Gore was attaching a long cable
to a socket in the base.
The other end of the cable
was plugged into the

Monster Megacharger.

Miss Fitt's eyes flicked open.

"Vampires!" she muttered—too quietly for Mr. Gore to hear, but loudly enough to startle the bats.

"Ouch!" said Boris, walloping his head on the machine.

"Now!" yelled Gore. "It is time!"

"Oh no!" cried Bella. "Look! We're too late!"

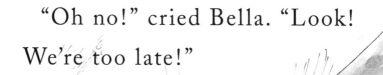

FLA-AA-SH! KERRR-BOOOM!

A stupendous bolt of lightning struck the conductor with a great *BANG*!

As the thunder exploded overhead, brilliant blue sparks flashed down the conductor, along the cable, into the Monster Megacharger, out through the

wires—and into the bolts in
Miss Fitt's neck. She jerked and
twitched and bounced into the
air, nearly snapping her straps.

"Come on!" hissed Lee.
"Time to get out of here!"

The bats darted into the
rafters just as Gore swung
around and lurched back toward
the bench.

"It is done! It is done!" wailed Gore, switching off the Monster Megacharger. "Zose pesky vampires do not know vot is comink! Hrurgh! Hrurgh! Hrurgh!"

As old Gore cackled hysterically, the bats shot out of the attic and into the stormy sky.

"Well, that was a waste of time," said Lee gloomily.

"And now Miss Fitt will be even more horrble," said Bella.

"I'm going home to get out

of the rain," shivered Billy.

"Me too," said Lee.

"And me," said Bella. "See you both at school later—"

She suddenly hesitated.

"Hang on," she gasped. "Where's Boris?"

Chapter 7
After the Storm

Before lessons the next
evening, Lee and Bella told
everyone about their adventure
in old Gore's attic.

"What?" said Big Herb,
between chomps of chocolate
Screme Egg. "You mean
old Gore has made
Miss Fitt even worse?
How can she be
worse than she was
yesterday? It took
me so long to do

my math homework, I didn't get into my coffin till it was almost daylight."

"We don't know what happened to Boris," said Bella. "I hope he didn't have to spend the whole day hiding in the attic from old Gore and Miss Fitt!"

STOMP! STOMP! STOMP! STOMP!

"Yikes," said Lee. "Here she comes! Where's Billy?"

"He's late," said Bella. "Miss Fitt will go ballistic!"

As the stomping got closer, Mr. Gore suddenly appeared with his tool bag and pretended to check the classroom door, which was still broken from the night before. But he kept glancing at the class and chuckling unpleasantly.

"Look at him," whispered Lee. "He's waiting to see the results of the Monster Megacharger."

STOMP! STOMP! STOMP! STOMP!

A few seconds later, Miss Fitt stood in the doorway.

"Good mornink, Miss Fitt!"
smarmed Gore. "Anysink you
need, Your Monstrosity, just
let me
know!"

Miss Fitt stomped to the
front of the class. And just at
that moment, Billy hurtled
through the door.

The whole class gasped
in horror. Poor Billy! What
would Miss Fitt do?

Mr. Gore smirked and rubbed his hands together in glee. Little flakes of finger snowed down onto his boots.

"I-I'm really s-sorry I'm late, miss!" panted Billy in terror.

Miss Fitt stared at him.

"M-my watch stopped," said Billy. "I-it got wet in the rain."

The other children held their breath. No one dared to move.

Miss Fitt opened her mouth.

And smiled.

"Never mind, Billy," she chuckled. "These things happen. Just run along and sit down. That's a good boy."

The whole class gasped again —in disbelief.

"S-sorry, miss?" said Billy, not quite daring to move.

"I do hope your watch can be mended," Miss Fitt went on. "Perhaps Mr. Gore would be kind enough to look at it for you?"

Mr. Gore had stopped rubbing his hands together. His mouth

had fallen open, and he was making a strange gurgling sound.

"Dear me, are you all right, Mr. Gore?" said Miss Fitt. "You look a little green."

"That's just his normal color!" whispered Lee to Bella.

"I-I'm . . . fine," croaked Mr. Gore. "But you . . . you're supposed to be . . . I thought . . . "

"Oh good," interrupted Miss Fitt firmly. "I'm delighted

you're well. Now do be a
dear and fix Billy's watch. By
lunchtime?"

Billy handed over his watch.
He still couldn't quite believe
what was happening. Nor
could anyone else.

Mr. Gore glared at Billy
and stuffed the watch into his
overalls.

"Good-bye, Mr. Gore!" said Miss Fitt brightly.

Old Gore shuffled out of the classroom, muttering very rude things about vampires.

Billy sat down next to Lee and Bella.

"Wow! What's happened to Miss Fitt?" he whispered.

"No idea," shrugged Lee. "Pretty cool though, isn't it?"

"Mmm," said Bella. "Let's see what she's like in math first."

"Now then, class," said Miss Fitt. "Today we shall start

with . . . But what are you doing, my dears?"

"Getting out our math books, miss," said several glum voices at once.

"Math?" said Miss Fitt. "Really?"

She checked the timetable.

"Good gracious!" she said. "Who on earth has been making you do so much math? Dear me. This will never do!"

Miss Fitt grabbed an eraser and rubbed out all her changes from the night before. Then

she crossed out all the normal
math lessons and wrote
EXTRA BREAK instead.

"I find math so terribly
dull," said Miss Fitt. She took
a brown paper bag out of her
handbag. "Now, who would
like some candy?"

At lunchtime, the first thing
Lee, Bella, and Billy did was
turn into bats and zoom up

to the clock tower. They were relieved to find Boris safe and well.

"What happened last night?" said Lee. "Why didn't you follow us out of the attic?"

"Well," began Boris. "Remember when Miss Fitt woke up and said 'Vampires'?"

"Oh yeah," said Lee. "That was really freaky."

"I know!" said Boris. "I got such a fright, I whacked my head on one of the knobs on the Monster Megacharger. It was behind some wires, and I hadn't noticed it before. When I looked closer, I saw the knob was marked *Horrometer*."

"Hey!" said Billy. "That's the special knob I was looking for!"

"The Horrometer had ten settings," Boris went on. "From one, Sweet and Nice, to ten, Scary and Nasty. The knob was set to number ten, but I had just enough time to switch it to one before the lightning struck the conductor."

"Fantastic!" said Lee. "So

Miss Fitt got a super-duper double dose of NICENESS!"

"That's right," said Billy. "Old Gore must have changed her setting."

"Hang on," wondered Lee. "That still doesn't explain why you didn't leave the attic when we did."

"I got a bit tangled in the wires," said Boris. "By the time I freed myself, old Gore was heading my way, so I hid behind the machine until he went to bed. Then I just flew back here."

Just above their heads, the school clock struck one.

"One o'clock! Yikes, we'd better get back and eat lunch," said Lee.

"Do you know what?" said Billy. "Miss Fitt gave us so much candy, I don't think I can manage my raw steak sandwich."

"Oh, just give it to Big Herb," laughed Bella.

"Bye, Boris," called Lee as they fluttered out of the clock tower. "And thanks for saving us from two whole weeks of math!"

hungry for more?

Sink your teeth into the next
Vampire School adventure.

Vampire School
Stage Fright

St. Orlok's is ready for its big phantomime —*Snow Fright and the Seven Dwarfs*. The mummy, werewolf, zombie, and vampire parents are assembled. Bella is Snow Fright while Lee and Billy are two of the seven dwarfs—Gappy, Snappy, Flappy, Creepy, Chompy, Gnashful, and Shock. But after an exhausting lesson of swooping, swerving, and skulking, Bella isn't feeling very well. How will the show go on?

Vampire School
Casketball Capers

Lee, Billy, and Bella are all on the St. Orlok's casketball team. (That's the vampire version of basketball, in case you've never played it.) They're all getting ready for a big game against the Chaney Street werewolves. But when the other team arrives, it seems that some of them aren't planning on playing a fair game. Lee needs to come up with a plan—fast! Will he manage to foil the cheaters before the final whistle?

Vampire School
Ghoul Trip

Lee, Billy, and Bella and the rest of Miss Gargoyle's class are off on a school trip to the funfair. But when they arrive, there are some very strange characters hanging around. Could they have anything to do with the string of robberies that have been happening around town? Lee, Billy, and Bella decide to do some investigating and get to the bottom of the mystery.